PAW Patrol: Christmas Is Coming!

By Hollis James • Based on the teleplay by James Backshall and Jeff Sweeney

Illustrated by MJ Illustrations

Random House 🏠 New York

rhcbooks.com

ISBN 978-0-593-38081-9 (trade)

MANUFACTURED IN CHINA

10 9 8 7 6 5 4 3 2 1

Format development and production by Red Bird Publishing Ltd., UK

It was a few days before Christmas, and the pups were practicing their song for the upcoming Adventure Bay Holiday Spectacular. Ryder stopped by to see how they were doing.

"Everyone sounds great!" Ryder said.

"Thanks," said Skye. "I just hope it snows."

"It will," said Rubble. "It always snows for the Holiday Spectacular!"

"It sure would be fun for our visitors!" said Ryder.

The next day, it still hadn't snowed. Jake said that every time he washed his truck, it rained. So the pups began washing his truck. Maybe that would make it snow! Just then, Tracker and Carlos arrived.

Tracker, who had never seen snow before, noticed the bucket of suds.
"Is that snow?" he asked. "Look at it . . . it's so white and fluffy. *¡Nieve!* Snow!"
And before the pups could answer, he jumped right in!
"Tracker, wait!" Skye said. "That's not snow!"

Two days later, Mayor Goodway and her friends were preparing the stage for the Holiday Spectacular. Katie adjusted the lights and Mr. Porter delivered a carrot cake shaped like a snowman.

"Ha!" Mayor Humdinger said, pulling the carrot off the cake and taking a bite. "Looks like your snow will be a no-show for your Christmas show!"

"It still may snow!" said Mayor Goodway. "Besides, we have a lot more than that. Yum-a-licious food and fabulous entertainment, plus the PAW Patrol will be performing an original song. And we'll have some very special guests. . . ."

Just then, Cap'n Turbot arrived with three friends from the South Pole. "I present to you the performing penguins: Pete, Peggy, and Poindexter!"

Cap'n Turbot fed the penguins some squid jerky, and they started performing their skating routine.

"Wonderful!" said Mr. Porter.

"Indeed," Mayor Humdinger said to himself. "And I could make a fortune with them."

But not everyone was enjoying the penguins' routine. A member of the Kitten Catastrophe Crew was startled, which scared a penguin and sent everyone scurrying in all directions.

The stage quickly erupted in chaos. Lights fell down. The snowman cake was crushed. It took only a few seconds to undo the whole day's work.

Mayor Goodway immediately called the PAW Patrol.

"We're on it, Mayor Goodway," said Ryder. "No stage is too big, no pup is too small!"

Ryder and the pups raced to the scene and got to work. Rocky took Marshall's ladder up to the top of the stage and used his tools to secure a fallen beam. Tracker used his cables to lift the Christmas lights.

Just as the pups were finishing at the end of the day, it started to snow!

"Tomorrow's Holiday Spectacular is going to be the best ever!" said Rubble.

The next morning, everything was ready for the show. The stage was fixed, the snow was thick, and Mr. Porter had made a new cake.

But when Cap'n Turbot went out to his van to wake the performing penguins, he saw they were gone!

"Peggy, Pete, Poindexter!" yelled Cap'n Turbot. "Where'd you go?"

Mayor Humdinger had captured the penguins! But he was in for a big surprise.
"There's nothing amusing about skating in my hat!" he said. "Oh, kittens, make them stop!"
But the kittens couldn't control them. The penguins escaped into the snow with the kittens chasing after them.

The PAW Patrol got a call from Mayor Humdinger, who told them the penguins had escaped into Foggy Bottom Forest with his kitties.

"We've got to rescue them in time for tonight's Holiday Spectacular," said Ryder. "It's almost showtime!"

They raced into the woods, where the snow was heavy and the wind was fierce.

"We must be close," said Ryder, squinting into the icy air. "But instead of looking for them, why don't we get the penguins to look for us?"

Ryder put some squid jerky on the end of Rubble's crane. Once the penguins smelled the treats, they came running—and the kittens were interested, too!

Back in Adventure Bay, the Holiday Spectacular had begun! While the audience was waiting for the performing penguins, Chickaletta played her keyboard . . .

Carlos performed magic . . .

and Jake played a song on his tuba!

Meanwhile, in Foggy Bottom Forest, the PAW Patrol was lost!
"I can't see through this snow," Ryder said. "And my GPS isn't working."
Then Tracker said, *"Por favor, amigos,* please be quiet. I hear something. . . ."
He listened closely with his super hearing. It sounded like . . . Jake's tuba!

The PAW Patrol followed the sound of tuba music back to the Holiday Spectacular.
Cap'n Turbot's performing penguins arrived just in time for the show!
Everyone cheered as the perky penguins danced and slid around the stage.

Not only did the PAW Patrol save the day in time for the Holiday Spectacular, but the pups' new winter song totally rocked the house!

"This is so exciting!" Skye exclaimed.

"Do you know what's even more exciting?" Rubble asked. "Tomorrow is Christmas!"

"Thank goodness," Skye replied. "I can barely wait another day."